February 14, 1997

APOLLO 13

The Junior Novelization

Library of Congress Cataloging-in-Publication Data
Anastasio, Dina. Apollo 13 : the junior novelization / adapted by Dina Anastasio ;
screenplay by William Broyles, Jr. & Al Reinert and John Sayles ; with photos from
NASA and the movie Apollo 13 ; based on the book Lost moon by Jim Lovell and Jeffrey
Kluger. p. cm. Summary: When their main oxygen tank explodes on the way to the
moon, the crew of Apollo 13 use their tiny lunar module as a lifeboat and hope to return
to earth. [1. Apollo 13 (Spacecraft)—Fiction. 2. Space flight to the moon—Fiction.
3. Spaceflight—Fiction. 4. Moon—Exploration—Fiction.] I. Lovell, Jim. Lost moon.
II. Title. PZ7.A5185Ap 1995 [Fic]—dc20 95-14173 CIP AC

ISBN 0-448-41120-2 A B C D E F G H I J

APOLLO 13

The Junior Novelization

Adapted by **Dina Anastasio**

From a motion picture written by
**William Broyles, Jr. & Al Reinert
and John Sayles**

Based on the book *Lost Moon* by
Jim Lovell and Jeffrey Kluger

Grosset & Dunlap
New York

A13 July 20, 1969

The rough, lonely surface of the moon had been waiting for a long, long time. Meteors may have brushed its dusty, craggy craters. Debris from the deepest regions of outer space may have pierced its dead exterior. But never before had life touched it. Not until now. Today, for the first time, footsteps would fall on the battered surface. Laughter would awaken its dead soul. For one tiny blink in the history of the universe, man would cast a shadow over the moon's lonely craters.

And then it happened. The astronaut Neil Armstrong, moved onto the top of the steps and looked around. He glanced down at the lunar surface, then turned and moved carefully down the ladder, grasping the railings with his bulky gloves. When he reached the bottom, he stopped.

As the world watched from their living rooms, the astronaut poised above the moon waited. The surface of the moon waited. And far away, seated in front of television sets back on Earth, Jim Lovell, Fred Haise, and Bill Anders, the Apollo 11 backup team, waited too. Each member of that team had hoped to be the first to step onto the moon. But it was not to be. They would not be first. But they knew that they would be there some day.

"Some day I'm going to take that step," Jim Lovell said to his youngest son, Jeffrey. They were sitting on the couch, staring at the television screen. Across the room, Jim's wife Marilyn frowned. For Jim's sake, she hoped that his words would come true. But she also dreaded each and every space mission.

Jim's other children, fifteen-year-old Jay, fourteen-year-old Barbara, and eleven-year-old Susan moved closer to the television set.

And then, over 200,000 miles above them, Neil Armstrong took the first step on the moon.

"That was one small step for man, one giant step for mankind," his voice crackled as it beamed through the universe to the people back home.

"Look at the rocks, Dad!" the five-year-old shouted. "Look at the moon rocks!"

"I see them, Jeffrey," Jim said, as the second astronaut emerged from the spacecraft. Buzz Aldrin stood at the top of the ladder for a second, then he too began to climb down.

"Are you really going to the moon?" Jeffrey turned to face his father. Jim Lovell had gone to the moon once before, but he had never walked on it. It had been the Apollo 8 mission, the first mission to circle the moon.

"It looks like it, Jeffrey," Jim said. "I'm told I'll be commanding the Apollo 14 mission to the moon. Pete Conrad will command the Apollo 12 mission. Then Alan Shepard will lead Apollo 13. And then it's my turn."

"And will you bring me a moon rock?"

"If there is any way that I can, I will."

"Do you promise?" Jeffrey asked.

Jim Lovell put his arm around his son.

Jim had been waiting for such a long time. But he knew that some day it would be his shadow passing over the moon.

"I promise," Jim whispered. "If there is any way at all, I will bring you a moon rock."

The wait was almost over. No more watching. No more second best. The crew of Apollo 13 was going to the moon.

In November of 1969, Alan Shepard had developed an ear infection, and Jim Lovell was chosen to replace him as commander of the mission. Fred Haise would be the lunar module pilot. And Ken Mattingly would be in charge of the command module. Now, just nine days before lift-off, the three astronauts were preparing to cast their own shadows across the golden circle.

Inside the command module simulator, the crew concentrated on the control panel in front of them. The command module simulator was exactly like the command module that would take them to the moon. In it, they could practice every possible maneuver, preparing themselves for any event. Then, when it was time to go inside the actual spacecraft, they would be ready . . . for anything.

Right now, they were practicing docking

the command module to the lunar excursion module, or LEM for short. Nose to nose. Docking was a way of connecting the two vehicles so that the astronauts could move from one into the other.

The astronauts had decided on the name *Odyssey* for their command module. It would be a long voyage, and the word "odyssey" meant just that. The command module would be their home until it was time to land on the moon. Then, while Ken stayed in the command module, Jim and Fred would enter the LEM and pilot it down to the moon's surface.

They had decided to call their lunar module *Aquarius*, after the Egyptian goddess who was thought to have brought life and knowledge to the Nile valley in Egypt. In the same way, the astronauts hoped, *Aquarius* would bring life to the moon, and knowledge to the people on Earth.

Ken took over the simulator's controls and went to work. Right now, this was his ship. He would have to pilot it while the others were performing their scientific experiments on the moon. He watched the blip that represented the LEM shake on the screen in front of him. The trick was to line up that blip between the crosshairs of the screen. If he could catch it right on the cross, the maneuver would be perfect.

"Houston, we're at one hundred feet and closing," Fred reported over his radio. Fred's job was to read the measurements on the panel in front of him and communicate them to the other astronauts and to Mission Control.

"You're looking good," Mission Control answered.

"Seventy-five feet and closing," Fred announced. "Coming up on docking, Houston."

The Houston controllers turned off their mikes. "Let's blow the aft thrusters on him," one of them suggested.

The other controller nodded in agreement.

It was a test, a simulated test to see the astronauts' response to an emergency situation. If it didn't work, it would be all right . . . this time. But if it didn't work later, when they were in space, it could be a disaster. Better to correct any problems now.

With a flip of a switch, the controller turned off the aft thrusters, the engines on the command module's rear.

Suddenly, the LEM seemed to veer to the right.

"Whoa! I lost something!" Ken announced. "I can't translate left."

"We're losing altitude, Houston," Fred said.

"Barber poles on two isolation valves," Jim suggested. "Try recycling the valves."

"There isn't time for that!" Ken insisted.

"Let me recycle the valves!" Jim said.

"No! I got it. I got it."

"Ten feet." Fred was watching the controls carefully. The lunar module was closing into the center of the crosshairs.

"Ten feet," Ken announced. The LEM was lining up perfectly. He could feel the command module simulator respond to his every touch, as if it were part of his body.

Ken hit a button and listened as the machine simulated a solid THUNK.

"We have capture, Houston," Ken shouted.

"Beautiful maneuver, *Odyssey*," the controller answered. "You guys are quick."

But Ken didn't think it was perfect. This was one of the most important maneuvers of the flight, and it had to be exactly right. During launch, the LEM rode behind the command module. Once they were in space, the LEM had to be repositioned so that it was nose to nose with the command module and accessible to the astronauts.

If Ken didn't line his ship up exactly, instead of docking with the LEM, the command module's probe could puncture the lunar module's thin foil skin, making it unuseable for a moon landing.

Ken shook his head and sat back in his couch. "I want to do it again," he said, as the others left the simulator. "My rate of turn seems too slow. Listen guys, I want to work it again."

Fred and Jim were used to it. Nothing was ever good enough for Ken. Sometimes it was annoying, but it was also why Ken was one of the best pilots in the program.

But Jim was tired. "I've had it," he sighed. "And I find I'm a better pilot when I can keep my eyes open. I'm going home to see my family."

"Jeffrey's been waiting for you," Marilyn Lovell said after she had kissed her husband hello.

"Where's everybody else?" Jim asked.

Marilyn nodded toward the living room. "Watching TV. Jeffrey's gone to bed, but he has so many questions, I doubt if he's asleep. Better go see him."

Jeffrey was sitting on his bed, wide awake. He wanted to know everything Jim had been doing. He wanted to know about the moon. He wanted to know how it would feel to be shot into the sky on the top of a huge rocket. He wanted to know how they would pick up his moon rock.

Jim sat down on the bed.

"What's that?" Jeffrey asked, pointing to the plastic models Jim was holding.

Jim held up the two pieces. One was a model of the command module. Attached to that was a tiny plastic LEM. "This is the spaceship that will take me to the moon," Jim said. "I thought we could have a little lesson here."

9

"Oh, yes!" Jeffrey nodded excitedly. "How long will it take you to get to the moon?"

"Only four days," said Jim. "Let me show you how this works. . . . First the Saturn 5 booster shoots us away from the earth."

"I know. Like a bullet in a gun."

"Right. BOOM! Off we go, straight up into space. As you know, the earth's gravity holds all things, all people, all everything, down. It keeps us from floating off into space. But that rocket is more powerful than even the earth's gravity.

"Now, about five-sixths of the way to the moon, the earth's gravity stops dragging on us and slowing us down and the moon's gravity starts pulling on us, speeding us up. Then, we go into orbit—a kind of circle— around the moon."

Jim pulled, and with a "pop" he detached the spidery lunar module from the cone-shaped command module.

"Okay," he said. "This is the LEM, which we named the *Aquarius*. After we orbit the moon, it leaves the command module, which we named the *Odyssey*." Jim held up the other model. "And like a rowboat leaving a ship, the *Aquarius* carries two of us down to the moon. Mr. Haise and myself. That's what it's for, and that's all it's for. The rest of the time we're in the command module.

"Actually, there's a third module, too. It's called the service module, and it carries lots of things that we need. Things like fuel, oxygen, power lines, and life-support equipment. Important stuff. The command module sits on top of the service module, but we never go inside it.

"Anyway, back to the LEM. Remember when Neil Armstrong landed on the Sea of Tranquillity? Well, Mr. Haise and I are going to land in an entirely new place on the moon, called the Fra Mauro. It's a very hilly place, which will make landing interesting, and the rock samples we get will be completely new. We'll explore the hills, and then we'll collect rocks for all those geologists waiting at home.

"While we're down on the moon, Ken Mattingly will stay in the *Odyssey* and circle the moon."

Jim took a deep breath and continued. "Once we've completed our experiments, I'll pilot the LEM back up and Ken will kind of spear us with the *Odyssey*. We call that docking. That's what we've been practicing for the past few days."

Jeffrey stared up at his father. "What if something breaks, Dad?"

"Then we have what are called our backup systems, like a spare tire on your car. Remember Jeffrey, I've been practicing for this trip for a long, long time. We've been over and over everything that could possibly happen."

Jeffrey's face looked worried.

"Don't worry, Jeffrey," Jim said, putting his arm around his son, "I'm a very lucky guy. And I think 13 will be a very lucky mission." *It better be*, thought Jim. *There sure are a lot of thirteens involved.* The Apollo 13 astronauts would be lifting off at 1:13 P.M.—thirteen hundred hours and thirteen minutes, military time. And on April thirteenth, they were scheduled to enter the moon's gravitational field.

"Everything will be just fine," Jim promised. "And don't you forget it."

Jeffrey laughed a relieved laugh. "I won't," he said. "As long as you don't forget my moon rock."

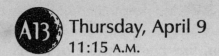
Jim was talking to a technician when the flight surgeon walked over. Nearby, the 363-foot Saturn rocket was being readied on the launchpad. In two days, that rocket would send him into outer space.

The doctor did not look happy at all. "Bad news, Jim," the flight surgeon said. "I just got some blood work back from the lab. I'm afraid one of your backups has the measles."

Jim shrugged. "So? They're not going with us."

"It means you've all been exposed," the doctor explained.

Jim's eyes widened as he tried to remember if he'd ever had the measles. Of course he had. How could he forget. He could almost feel the itching.

"I had the measles when I was a kid," he said.

The flight surgeon shook his head. "But Ken Mattingly hasn't."

Jim's whole body tensed. "So what? So what if he hasn't had the measles? That doesn't mean he'll get it." Jim was practically shaking. But there was no point in taking it out on the doctor, Jim knew. All he did was read the tests.

Jim turned quickly and headed toward the office of the NASA director.

"What does this mean?" he asked breathlessly, when he was in front of the director's desk.

"It means we have a serious problem."

"You're going to break up my crew two days before launch? When we know each other's moves and we can read the tone of each other's voices?"

"Ken is going to get seriously ill, Jim." The voice belonged to the flight surgeon. He had followed Jim in and was standing by the office door. "His blood test shows he might already be fighting off the disease. He could develop full-blown measles during the mission, which means he would get ill just as you and Haise are returning from the lunar surface. You will be returning from the moon with a LEM full of moon rocks and scientific material, and he will be in the command module scratching. He will be itching. He will be very, very sick, Jim."

"Who's going to take his place?"

"Jack Swigert."

Jim thought about Jack Swigert. Jack had hardly even been near the simulator. Now he had less than forty-eight hours to prepare for their maneuvers. Would he have time to learn what it meant when Jim raised his voice, or lowered it, or cleared his throat in a certain way? Jim knew he could trust Ken Mattingly with his life. But Jack . . . ?

"He is fully qualified to fly this mission," the director said.

"He's a good pilot," Jim agreed. "But he's only had a *fraction* of Ken's time in the simulator!"

"Either we scrub Mattingly and go with Swigert, or we bump all of you to a later mission."

Jim knew what that meant. If they were bumped now, there was a very good possibility that none of them would get the chance again.

"But we only have two days till launch!" Jim was furious.

But the flight director was firm. "If you hold out for Ken, you won't be on Apollo 13."

Jim knew it was no use. They would have

to go without Ken. Somehow, they'd have to get Jack ready. Somehow, they'd have to manage.

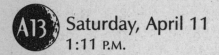 Saturday, April 11
1:11 P.M.

Two days later, Jim Lovell, Fred Haise, and Jack Swigert entered an elevator at the launch-pad in Cape Kennedy, Florida. It was a fine, warm Saturday in April. The astronauts were dressed in bulky space suits that would keep their body temperatures at a normal level in space. On their heads were helmets. Tiny wires that would allow the doctors on the ground to monitor their heart rates were glued to their skin.

They were ready.

The elevator carried them up to the command module, past the 363-foot-tall Saturn rocket that would propel them into space. Black fuel lines snaked from the bottom. Red stabilizers stuck out from the sides like arms. Vapor spewed off the rocket in huge puffs. It seemed like a dragon, alive and angry. As the astronauts scaled the rocket in silence, they were all thinking the same thing. Four million pounds of high explosives—enough to shoot them out of the earth's atmosphere. That's what they would be sitting on.

Jim Lovell had done it before. But the others hadn't. This was his fourth trip into space. And it was his second on top of the Saturn 5 rocket.

When the Apollo 8 spacecraft had been blasted toward the moon a little over a year before, the Saturn 5 rocket had done the job. It had been the Saturn's first flight, and Jim Lovell's third.

And now he was going to do it again.

Jim studied the other two astronauts. They seemed relaxed. But Jim wondered if they really were. He remembered his first flight into space. He had tried to seem nonchalant, but he had been more than a little nervous. Who wouldn't be?

The elevator jerked to a stop, and the astronauts entered the command module. They knew it well. They had practically lived in a simulator exactly like it for months. They knew every inch of the ship by heart.

One by one, the astronauts slid into their

couches—actually they were more like hammocks, lined up near the front of the command module. No cushions would be needed when they reached zero gravity.

Jim was in the commander's couch on the left. Jack was in the middle. And Fred was in the couch on the right. On the floor by their feet was the lower equipment bay where they could store their pressure suits and helmets once they were out of Earth orbit. And directly in front of their couches was the lifeblood of the ship: the instrument panel. It contained more that five hundred controls, with buttons large enough to be pushed by fingers wearing huge gloves.

Strapped in at last, the astronauts checked the instrument panel and watched as the hatch was lowered and sealed. Then they sat back and waited.

They did not have long. In less than two minutes, it would be 1:13.

Inside the Mission Control room in Houston, Texas, the controllers were counting down. On the huge screen in the front of the room, the Saturn rocket sat poised on the ground.

"We're go."

"Go, Flight."

"Go for launch."

"Go."

Gene Kranz, the flight director, listened as his controllers reported their status. Then he called over the radio to the launch center in Florida. "Launch control, this is Houston. We are go for launch."

"Roger that, Houston," the launch director replied from Florida. "Tower security, what's your status?"

"Go in one minute thirty seconds," the director of launch operations answered.

The world stood ready, its body tensed. In the bunker pad beside the huge rocket, the excited ground crew chanted off the seconds. The bunker shook with anticipation.

Only one person was quiet. On the far side of the room, Ken Mattingly stood alone: the man left behind.

Inside the command module, the three astronauts were counting down too.

"Get ready for the kickoff, fellas," Jim Lovell laughed as the seconds ticked away. "Just a couple of little bumps and we're in orbit."

"We're go to launch," the launch director announced. "T–minus twelve, eleven, ten, nine, eight, seven, six, five, four, three, two, one, lift-off!"

Suddenly, a volcano of flame erupted downward from the engines in the Saturn rocket. Far below the astronauts, the rocket was going to work. Its one and only job was to shoot the astronauts out of the earth's atmosphere. An ear-splitting roar shook the command module. As Fred and Jack gripped their seats, Jim Lovell grinned. The rocket was beginning to rise!

Like wet, discarded robes, the sheets of ice that had been cooling the rocket fell off. The black, snakelike fuel lines blew away. The enormous arms that held them down let go. And the rocket moved upward. To those who were watching, it looked like a giant sky-scraper climbing toward the heavens on a pedestal of flame and steam.

"Houston, we have cleared the tower," the launch director announced, as the huge rocket shot through the Florida sky.

"Roger that," Kranz answered from Houston. "Okay, guys. It's ours now."

The launch center's job was finished. From now on, Kranz and his team in Houston would be following the astronauts.

On the screen in front of Kranz, the rocket muscled its way up through the clear blue sky, accelerating at an incredible rate. The rocket seemed to grow smaller as it moved toward the horizon, until a trail of thick smoke was all that was visible.

Inside the command module, the astronauts were rocking and rolling from side to side, as the engines adjusted.

"Get ready for a little jolt," Jim warned the others. Then the rocket flame cut off and the acceleration suddenly stopped. It was more than a little jolt, however. The sudden deceleration sent the astronauts flying forward against their straps. It was almost as if the ship had smashed into a wall.

Below them, the Saturn's giant first stage fell away and the second stage engines ignited. Flames shot through the sky, as the newly powered rocket slammed the astronauts back into their seats.

"Wow!" Jack said. "That was some little jolt!"

"Stage two ignition, Houston," Jim reported calmly.

The voice of Mission Control answered back from Houston. "Roger that, Jim. Right on time."

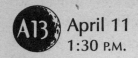
Jim glanced at the array of dials and lights in front of him. The whole panel was vibrating wildly. The five booster engine lights, normally arranged in an X, began to blur. Then, suddenly, the light in the center of the X began to blink and fade.

"This is *Odyssey*, Houston." Jim's tension was rising, despite his calm voice. "We've got a center engine cut-off. Go on the other four."

Jack and Fred turned to look at Jim through their visors as he spoke.

"Roger that, 13," Mission Control replied. "We've got the same."

Inside the command module, Jim and the others waited for the word back from Houston. Silently, they watched the control panel. The light in the middle remained black. Beside it, another button caught their attention. The word "ABORT" was written on it. It was not flashing. It was not shining. It was just there, waiting, in case the mission had to be stopped.

Jim wondered if they would have to abort

the mission because of the failed engine. If so, this was the button he would have to push. He closed his eyes and waited. He did not want to cancel the flight. He had waited too long already for his chance to walk on the moon. *Please*, he thought, *let's carry on.*

"Houston, what's the story on engine five?" he said into his radio finally.

"Can you confirm engine five out?" Flight Director Kranz asked one of his engineers.

"Roger that. It shut down early."

"Is that a problem?" Kranz asked.

"Yes, but press on. As long as we don't lose another one we'll be all right."

With that, Kranz radioed back up to the waiting astronauts. "We're not sure why the inboard was out early, but the other engines are GO, and you are *GO*," Kranz called back.

"Roger that," Fred answered.

Jim said a silent thank-you and smiled. "Looks like we've had our problem for this mission."

Outside the command module, the sky had darkened. The ship had slowed. The launch had been successful. They were in space—102 miles above the earth.

Now they would orbit the earth for a few

hours, just to make sure the ship was fit for the voyage ahead. Then they would relight the Saturn's third stage engines that would shoot them toward the moon.

"Apollo, this is Houston. Stand by for shutdown."

Before Jim had a chance to answer, the acceleration quit. The roar that had taken them into space faded into silence. They were airborne. Outside, the second stage rocket floated away into the black of space. Inside, as zero gravity began to take effect, a notebook floated eerily around the module. A pair of loose screws floated out of their holes and drifted past Jim's shoulder. Shifting his weight, Jim snapped off his helmet and held it tightly so that it would not float away.

"Gravity!" he muttered.

"You mean no gravity," Fred laughed. "I guess it's one of those things that you just take for granted. Like breathing. Life sure is harder without it."

Jim nodded and glanced out of the window at the blue-green ocean far below. A moment later it was gone, replaced again by the blackness of space.

They floated gently, orbiting the earth and readying their ship. Now and then they took turns snapping pictures of the universe around them.

"We're coming up on sunrise now, Houston," Jim reported. "It looks like a wonderful rainbow at midnight. I wish you folks could see it."

"It's a beautiful sight," Fred added.

Inside Mission Control, Kranz was staring at the screen in front of him. A dotted line showed the path of the Apollo spacecraft. The spacecraft had just about finished its second circle around the earth. A clock ticked off the time of the flight. 2:34:22.

"All command module systems go for TLI," a mission controller announced. TLI stood for "translunar injection." The injection was really a shot of power that would aim the spacecraft directly toward the moon.

"Third stage reignition in one minute twenty."

"Tell them they are a go for TLI," Kranz said. "Okay, fellas, we're going to the moon."

Within seconds, the Saturn's S-IVB engine ignited. Flames trailed as the spacecraft shot through space. Inside, Jim Lovell was grinning. It was great to be back!

The earth faded swiftly, as the *Odyssey* headed for the moon. It was a nice ride compared to the earlier g-filled jolts from stages one and two.

"Ten seconds to shutdown," Fred announced.

Ten seconds later, the engines shut down, and the spacecraft floated on its own toward the moon. Now came the moment they had been practicing for so intently.

"*Odyssey*, we are go for docking," Mission Control reported from Houston.

Jack leaned toward the panel and pressed a button with the letters CSM-SEP on it. Slowly the command and service modules separated from the third stage and began to float freely through the vacuum of space. Gracefully they turned, until the *Odyssey's* nose was facing the rocket stack. As they turned, the astronauts could see the rocket's panels fall away to reveal its precious cargo—the spidery LEM, *Aquarius*.

The LEM actually carried two stages, or engines. On the bottom was the descent stage. This engine would send Jim and Fred down to the moon. Below that stage were the four spindly legs that would stand the LEM on the moon. On top of the LEM was the ascent stage. This engine would lift them back off the moon and up to Jack in the waiting command module.

Jim glanced out of the window of the command module. Outside, the LEM was floating closer. It reminded Jim of a twenty-three-foot bug. He turned to Jack and eyed him nervously.

This was the maneuver that Ken had been working on for weeks in the simulator. It would be tricky. And now it was Jack's job to attach the nose of the command module to the top of the LEM. After that, they could disconnect what was left of the Saturn rocket and get on with their journey to the moon.

"Don't worry, Jim," Jack assured his commander. "I'm on top of it."

Jim nodded and turned back to the window. He wished that he had more confidence in Jack. But Ken Mattingly had been his partner for so long. He had watched Ken practice this maneuver over and over. But Jack had only had two days of practice.

"Five hundred feet to docking," Fred announced.

Outside the window, the LEM was getting closer.

"Two hundred feet," Fred said, studying the panel.

Jack leaned forward and squinted through the crosshairs in his optical sight. He was looking for matching lines on the LEM.

"Got it!" Jack muttered, as the crosses lined up. "Sixty feet to go."

The command module slid closer to the LEM, then closer and closer still. Finally they came together with a solid BANG. The LEM was secure. The two ships were now one.

"Houston, we have LEM capture," Jim announced. His body began to relax. He had to admit, Jack had done a nearly perfect job.

"We copy that, *Odyssey.*"

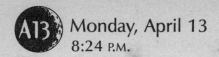 Monday, April 13
8:24 P.M.

"When's Dad coming on?" Jeffrey Lovell asked. He was standing beside his mother and his sisters in the Mission Control viewing room, along with the families and friends of the other two astronauts.

The huge screen in the front of the room was blank. But soon Jeffrey's father would be speaking to them from space. None of the television networks had decided to carry this broadcast. Not one. Not this time. So this was definitely the place to be. Jeffrey was just sorry that his brother Jay, away at military school, would not get to see it.

"Any minute now," Jeffrey's mother told him.

"Do you think he's all right?" Jeffrey asked nervously.

"He's fine," she assured him. "There's one thing to remember about space. If something goes wrong, you'll know it. This place would be going crazy. It's not, so nothing's gone wrong, and there's no reason to worry."

That's what Jeffrey's father had said, too.

29

But it was still hard not to worry.

"Wait! Look! There he is!" Jeffrey shouted, as the screen came to life.

The image of his father flashed onto the monitor at the front of the room. Jeffrey moved toward it and settled on the floor. A moment later, his father grinned into the camera and began to speak.

"Good evening, America," Jim said. "Welcome to Apollo 13. We're broadcasting live from an altitude of almost two hundred thousand miles. Tonight we're going to give you a little demonstration of what we do here in outer space. My crewmates, Fred Haise and Jack Swigert, are going to show you a few of our more domestic chores.

"Okay, let's start with cooking. Obviously, we have to eat up here in space, and cooking isn't easy in zero gravity. You quickly realize that apples do not fall to the ground up here. Or, they wouldn't if we had some. They float."

Jeffrey inched closer to the screen and tried to see what his father had in his hand. It was a plastic bag of dried food.

"We carry bags of dehydrated food," Jim said. "That means all the water's taken out.

But we have to put the water back in, or they would taste terrible."

As Jeffrey watched, Fred appeared on the television screen next to Jim. He was holding a water gun attached to a long hose. Jim handed Fred the bag of dry food and moved out of the way.

"Watch this!" Fred shouted, as he pointed the water gun at the package and fired. "Instant dinner! We don't cook so much as just add hot water. Now, I'm going to be the first man to eat grits in space."

"The first and the last," Jack added.

A few globules of water escaped from the package and wobbled in front of Jack's nose. He poked at them with his finger.

The camera shifted back to Jim. "Now, we're going to give you a tour of the lunar module, *Aquarius*," he said. "Fred, why don't you lead the way."

Fred nodded and began to swim through the air. Kicking his feet, he paddled through the tunnel that led from the command module to the LEM. Jim was right behind him. When they were inside the lunar module, Fred turned toward the camera.

"Welcome to the *Aquarius*," he said. "We're

not going to be able to power it up for you. But I can show you some of the more important features.

"As you can see, the lunar module is about the size of two telephone booths. In other words, it's small. Luckily, we don't have to spend too much time here. Just a quick trip down to the moon, and a quick trip back up. The walls separating us from the vacuum of space are only as thick as three pieces of thin aluminum foil."

Fred picked up a pen, a food bag, and a flashlight. He let them all go at exactly the same moment, and laughed as they spun around in front of his nose.

"That's called space juggling," he announced.

Fred and Jim drifted about the lunar module for a few more minutes. Then they headed back toward the tunnel that led to the command module.

"So," Jim announced, "we'll be closing out *Aquarius* and moving back to *Odyssey* now. Our next broadcast will be from the surface of the moon. This is the crew of Apollo 13, wishing everyone on Earth a nice evening."

"Don't forget my moon rock, Dad," Jeffrey

called, as the image of his father faded from the huge screen.

He felt better now. He wasn't as worried as he had been. His father was just fine. Maybe the number thirteen was lucky after all.

 **April 13**
9:07 P.M.

Jim shut off the TV camera and closed his eyes. He could relax now. It was the thirteenth of April, Monday night, Earth time, and the broadcast had gone well—despite the fact that no networks had shown it. There were still two more days to go before they reached the moon.

Inside the command module, the radio was crackling. "Excellent show, *Odyssey*," Mission Control said.

"Thank you, Houston," Jack answered.

"Now we've got a couple of little housekeeping procedures for you here," Mission Control continued. "We'd like you to roll right to 060 and null your rates. Then, if you could give your oxygen tanks a small stir."

"Roger that," Jack said. "I'm on it."

Without thinking much about it, Jack got ready to stir the two oxygen tanks back in the service module. It was a routine procedure, designed to keep the supercooled oxygen moving through the ship's fuel and ventilation systems. With a quick flip of a switch, heated coils inside the tank would stir up the thick gas. It was a simple thing to do.

Jack raised his index finger, and moved it toward the oxygen stir switch. Slowly, his finger flicked the switch for oxygen tank two, and . . .

"WHAT THE . . . !" Jim shouted, as he swam from the LEM into the command module. A thunderclap shook his entire body and sent him flying to the other side of the ship.

Jack sat frozen in his seat as the spacecraft quaked and shuddered violently around them. But it was Fred who actually saw the explosion move the ship and cause the walls of the LEM tunnel to buckle.

Then—WHOOM!—rivets and screws popped and a seam opened in the metal, and another explosion rattled the ship from one end to the other.

Warning lights blinked crazily across the instrument panel. No one had ever heard anything like it before.

Jim glanced at the others with wide, startled eyes. He wanted them to be smiling. He wanted it to be some kind of a joke.

But they weren't smiling. They were watching him with the same dumbfounded expression. He could tell that they had no idea what had happened, either.

Above Jack's head, a yellow warning light flashed "CREW ALERT!" and more flashing lights lit up the instrument panel. Alarms pierced through the tense spacecraft.

"Houston, we have a problem," Jack called over the radio.

"Say again," Mission Control answered.

Jim repeated the words as calmly as he could. "Houston, we have a problem."

The ship continued to lurch back and forth. Objects of all shapes and sizes tumbled and floated every which way.

Down at Mission Control, the flight surgeon watched the medical monitor.

"Their heart rates are skyrocketing!" he shouted.

"Oxygen tank number two is not reading at

all," a controller reported. "Number one tank is dropping."

Suddenly, every controller on the floor was barking out their own emergency reports.

"They're all over the place!"

"They keep yawing close to gimbal lock!"

"I keep losing radio signal!"

"Their antennae must be flipping around!"

"One at a time!" Gene Kranz announced. He was as nervous as anyone. But it was his job to keep everyone calm. Panic was the last thing they needed in an emergency situation. "Is this a problem with the instruments?" he quietly asked his electrical controller. "Or are we looking at real power loss up there?"

"If it is, it's a quadruple failure," came the answer. "But that can't happen. It's got to be the instruments!"

But it wasn't the instruments. Something was very wrong with the ship itself.

Two hundred thousand miles into space, the men in the *Odyssey* had even less of an idea of what was wrong with the ship. At first, Jim thought that a meteor must have hit the LEM; nothing is as frightening to an astronaut. In space, even a tiny bit of cosmic sand would feel and act like a speeding bowling ball.

"Get that hatch buttoned!" Jim instructed Jack. "The LEM may have taken a meteor."

Jack pushed his way to the tunnel and attempted to seal the hatch. After a moment, he turned, and called to the others. "I can't get this thing to seal!" he hollered.

"Forget it, then!" Jim shouted back. "If the LEM was hit, we'd be dead by now!"

Jim floated over to the side window and looked out. Something outside had caught his eye. Soon he realized what that something was. A thin, white, gassy cloud.

"See anything?" Fred asked.

"Boy, do I!" The cloud spread out around them for miles.

Jim pushed his way back to his seat and contacted Mission Control.

"Uh, Houston, it looks to me like we're venting something out into space."

As he spoke, the ship wobbled like a knuckleball. The command module shimmied from side to side, as the LEM gyrated in a circular motion. White crystals and metallic debris oozed from the side of the ship like ink from an octopus. Outside, the growing cloud of icy gas quickly filled the sky.

"I see it out of window one right now," Jim

reported. "It's a gas of some sort. It's got to be the oxygen. We've got a major leak here, Houston."

Mission Control knew that Jim was right. The cloud was oxygen. With the oxygen tanks reading virtually empty, and the knowledge that there was a leak somewhere, there was no other explanation.

"Roger, *Odyssey*," Mission Control answered. "We copy your venting."

Jim stared at the attitude indicator in front of him. The ship was drifting badly. And as long as the service module kept leaking oxygen, the ship would continue to drift.

"The oxygen two tank is already empty," he said. "And oxygen one is falling rapidly."

"Soon we're not going to have any power or oxygen at all," Fred added. "We're bleeding to death."

In Mission Control, the electrical controller turned to Kranz. "They've got to shut down the reactant valves on the fuel cells," he said.

"What will that do?" Kranz asked him.

The controller was ready with his answer. "If that's where the leak is, we can save what's left in the tanks. We could stabilize the ship and run it on the third fuel cell."

"But," Kranz said, "if we shut down the valves, there will be no way to open them again. We can't land on the moon with only one healthy fuel cell."

"Affirmative. The *Odyssey* is dying. This is the only option."

Kranz stared at the officer, speechless. Not land on the moon? There had to be another way. There must be something they could try . . . ?

The controller knew what Kranz was thinking.

"They'll die if we don't stop this leak," he said. "And we've got to do it fast."

It was up to Kranz. It was his decision. He thought hard before he answered. Then, finally, he said, "Let's have them close the reactant valves."

"Are you saying you want me to shut down the reac valves?" Jim asked when he heard the news. "Did I hear you right?"

"Yes Jim. We think closing the reac valves may stop the leak."

Jim couldn't speak. He understood too well the full impact of what Mission Control was saying. There would be no moon landing. Oxygen was their lifeline. Without it they would die. At this point they would be lucky to get home.

"Did you copy, Jim?" Mission Control asked.

"We copy, Houston," Jim replied huskily.

He glanced over at Jack and Fred, and turned off the mike.

"We just lost walking on the moon," he said.

 April 13
10:35 P.M.

Jim reached forward and flicked the two switches that would shut down the valves. Instantly, the two fuel gauges tumbled to zero. But the ship was still tumbling; the leak was not stopped.

"It didn't work," Jack reported. "I'm not going to have anything left in here to run the ship. Where's this leak coming from?"

As far as the astronauts could tell, there were only two hours left before the *Odyssey* would be out of oxygen. And since oxygen helped fuel the ship, they would also be out of power.

They were a very long way from home—over 200,000 miles. When the oxygen tank died, they would have three small batteries and one tiny oxygen tank left. They were their backups. They were meant to be used only at the very end of the flight. They could provide power for two hours. No more.

They had to do something—FAST! But what?

Suddenly Jim had an idea. The LEM had its own power supply. It was made to take two men to the moon and return them to the command module. But that was all it was made to do. It was not made to return to Earth. But maybe—just maybe—it could give them some time.

The Mission Controllers were thinking the same thing. "*Odyssey*," called Mission Control. "We need you to power down immediately, and you're going to have to power up the LEM at the same time. You'd better get somebody into the LEM."

"Fred's already on his way," Jim answered.

"You've got to get that LEM computer up, Jim. We've got some serious time pressure here."

"How long does it take you to power up

the LEM?" Jim called to Fred. Fred was seated at the controls of the LEM, studying his checklist.

"Three hours. That is, if we do everything according to the book."

"We're looking at less than fifteen minutes of life support left in the *Odyssey*," Mission Control explained.

Fred dropped the checklist in disbelief and watched as the booklet floated near his head.

Fifteen minutes! thought Jim. Now, for the first time, he was really discouraged. *Fifteen minutes? That was impossible.*

While the Apollo 13 astronauts were taking in the news, the Mission Control room was going crazy. More and more controllers were arriving, and Kranz was trying to keep everyone calm.

"All right, controllers," he said. "We've got to bring these guys home. And to do that, we need a computer to guide them. Jack is already using power from their reentry batteries just to stay alive. We have got to transfer the guidance system to the LEM—now. We have got to do it before the computer in the command module loses all its power. Or else . . ."

Kranz didn't have to finish. The controllers knew what he was thinking. They knew what it would mean if they lost the power in the command module computer before they could transfer the guidance system to the LEM's computer. It would mean the Apollo 13 astronauts could not fly their ship.

 **April 13**
10:45 P.M.

Inside the command module, the lights were beginning to flicker. The voices of the controllers were beginning to fade. Soon, only static would filter through the *Odyssey*'s radio. Jack was alone in the big ship now. Fred and Jim were in the LEM, preparing for the power shift.

Outside the window, the universe seemed endless. As he powered down the *Odyssey*, Jack felt lonelier than he had ever felt in his life. Strange, he thought, that he had come to this dying ship by accident. What an odd twist of fate.

"We're losing power fast," Jack said into

the radio. He was flipping through the pages of the checklist. "Did you say I should look at the pink pages?"

"Houston, I'm ready to power up the computer now," Jim called from inside the *Aquarius.*

"One at a time, guys," Mission Control answered. "You're both talking at once. For Jack, it's the pink pages. For Jim, on panel eleven, close the circuit breaker, then go to activation thirty."

Jack relayed some numbers, then stood by for more instructions from Houston. No one spoke. They were waiting for Jim to convert the numbers that Jack had given him.

"Ready, Jim?" Mission Control asked.

"Just a few more steps."

"We want to switch control to *Aquarius* now, Jack," the controller said. "Turn off all thrusters."

"Roger. I am powering down. I have no control at all," Jack answered. Then he reached for the switch that would power down the *Odyssey*'s final jets.

But Jim wasn't ready. "Hold on! Wait Houston! We don't have our corresponding system up yet . . ."

It was too late. Before Jim had a chance to finish his sentence, Jack hit the switch that turned off the command module's attitude-control thrusters. But the LEM's had not been powered up. Suddenly there was no way to balance the ship.

"We're not ready, Houston!" Jim cried, as the spacecraft began to tumble through space like a badly tossed football.

Outside the ship's window, the universe seemed to be spinning out of control. "There's no way to control this thing," Jim shouted through the LEM radio.

He gripped the stick and thrust it forward. Suddenly, the LEM lurched. "The command module is dragging us," Jim reported. "The control is out of whack."

"It feels like a runaway stagecoach," Fred added. His hands were shaking as he grabbed for something, anything, to hang onto.

The spacecraft was shimmying now. As the LEM thrusters popped on and off, it jerked and rolled one way, then the other.

"It's trying," Fred said.

"Trying what?" asked Jim.

"To right itself."

"The thrusters are fighting each other like crazy, Houston," Jim muttered over the radio. "But . . ." He was staring at the instrument panel in front of him. It was almost a perfect miniature of the one in the command module.

"But what, Jim?" The voice of Mission Control sounded tense.

"I think I've got it figured out, Houston." As he said the words, Jim could feel the ship begin to stabilize around him. "The LEM is the driver's seat now," he announced.

"Good to hear, *Aquarius*," Mission Control replied. "Can you read me, Jack?"

The static over in the command module was strong, but Jack could make out the Mission Controller's words. The panel in front of him was dark now. The only light left in the ship was coming from the computer screen directly in front of him.

"I've just got the computer screen here," Jack said.

"Shut her down, Jack," Mission Control told him.

"Do we know for sure that we can power this thing back up? It's gonna get awful cold in here."

Jack waited for an answer, but he heard nothing but static. He knew they still needed the *Odyssey* to get them home. The *Aquarius* could not reenter the earth's atmosphere. It had no heat shield to protect them from the violent heat they would encounter upon reentry—just those paper-thin walls. The idea of shutting off all the command module's power and jumping into the LEM was frightening. What if the command module froze so badly in subzero space that they couldn't defrost it? What if the batteries just wouldn't recharge?

But Jack also knew he had no choice. He raised his finger and pushed the button that said "OFF." The computer screen darkened. There was no light anywhere.

"We confirm shutdown, Jack," Mission Control announced. "Lunar module now in control."

"Roger that, Houston. This is *Odyssey* signing off."

Then, slowly, Jack took one last look around his dark ship and drifted down to the tunnel that would lead him into the LEM.

 April 13
11:00 P.M.

Room 210 of Mission Control was filling up.
Gene Kranz had called together his top controllers to try to figure out what to do. They
knew there was only enough water, power,
and oxygen in the LEM for two men for
forty-five hours—less than two days. No
more. Now they had to find a way to support
three men for three, four, or even five days—
as long as it took to get Apollo 13 back to
Earth.

And what about the engine of the command module? Would it refire? Or was it
now dead? What about the heat shield? Had
it been damaged? Would they burn up if they
tried to reenter the earth's atmosphere?

At last, Gene Kranz entered the room. The
men grew quiet as he began to speak.

"I want you to forget the manuals. From
this moment on we have a new mission. How
do we get our people home?"

"We just have to point them toward Earth
and shoot them home," someone suggested.

"No, no—we need to get them on a free

return trajectory." Another officer spoke up. "It's the safest way."

Kranz paced back and forth for a moment as he thought about that. "You mean use the moon's gravity to slingshot them around? That would take at least three days. But I have to agree."

Another controller shook his head. "There isn't time. The LEM can't support three men for that amount of time. We have to get them out of there fast. They should just turn around and power back home."

"What if there's been serious damage to the spacecraft?" someone else asked.

The room was silent for several moments. It was not a pleasant thought.

"Okay, hold it!" Kranz shook his head and began to pace again. "From what Lovell has told us, we may have had an explosion in the service module. Consider that engine gone. If we light that thing, it could blow the whole works. About the only thing the command module is good for is reentry. We're not leaving this up to chance. Free return trajectory is the only way."

The room was silent as Kranz let the news set in.

"Okay," he continued. "Once we come around the moon, we're going to need to fire up the LEM engine. It will give us some speed. Then we'll get back home as fast as possible."

"That engine was made to land on the moon," someone cried. "It wasn't made to do stuff like that!"

But Kranz wasn't worried about what the LEM was *designed* to do. He wanted to know what it *could* do.

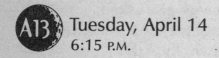 Tuesday, April 14
6:15 P.M.

It was almost time to go around the moon. Twenty-eight minutes. The crew of Apollo 13 would lose all radio contact with the earth for twenty-eight minutes while they went behind the moon and the moon itself blocked out their signals.

The astronauts were ready. Jim Lovell had done this before, inside Apollo 8. He was used to the absolute silence and darkness behind the moon. But this time was different.

This time the silence was edged with tension. It was more than just a quick, dark trip behind the moon. Who knew what might happen while they were out of contact with Mission Control?

Outside their window, the small blue earth slowly disappeared behind the dark moon.

"So long, Earth," Jack said softly. "Catch you on the flip side."

For the next half hour, the astronauts coasted through complete nothingness. Jim imagined the dark place below him where Neil Armstrong had taken man's first step on the moon. He could almost feel the sand that should have been shifting under his own feet.

And then, suddenly, a long arc of sun appeared in front of them. The rugged terrain of the moon was visible again. Desolate craters and gray hills passed by. For a moment, they thought they could make out their own landing site sixty miles below. Jim could almost see Jeffrey's lonely moon rock, resting in the whitish-gray dust.

"I'm sorry Jeffrey," Jim whispered. "Maybe next time."

Suddenly, the radio crackled, bringing Jim back to life. "Thirteen—this is Houston," a voice said. "It's good to see you guys again."

"Great to see you guys, too, Houston," Fred said.

Outside the window, Earth seemed to smile back at them as it rose over the edge of the moon. It was good to see it again. But would they ever *really* see it?

Jack focused his camera on the surface of the moon and snapped it. He'd come a long way. Maybe no one was going to walk on the moon. But at least he had seen it. And he'd have some photos to pass around, if . . .

"It's time," Jim said sternly.

Jack glanced at him and lowered his camera. He could see that Jim was edgy.

"I assume you want to live to develop those pictures," Jim said gravely. "So we'd better get on the stick. I want numbers on food and water. Do we have enough to get us home? Jack, bag up whatever water is left in the *Odyssey*, and bring it in here. It's going to freeze over there."

As Jack made his way into the *Odyssey*, Fred quickly checked the numbers. "If the engine fires like it's supposed to, the burn will speed us up by ten hours. But it'll still take us another three and a half days till splashdown. We'll have to cut way back on the water we drink."

"What about power?" Jim asked.

"Not even close. "

 April 14
8:40 P.M.

John Arthur, a young electrical controller, had been doing a lot of thinking about power. If anybody knew about electricity, it was Arthur. He stepped up to the front of Room 210 and faced Gene Kranz.

"It's as simple as this," he said. "Power is everything. If they run out of power, they can't talk to us. Without power they cannot fix their trajectory. What if they're off course? What if they're pointed toward Mars? Without power, they can't fix it. Which means that they could end up anywhere.

"Then they will need power to reenter the earth's atmosphere. If they are going to have enough for that, we have to shut their power off NOW. They're sucking it up by the minute. Everything has to go."

"What do you mean, 'everything'?" Kranz asked.

"I mean everything. The LEM is drawing sixty amps. At this rate, the LEM batteries will be dead in sixteen hours."

"I thought we had fifty-five hours," Kranz said.

"We don't. We have sixteen hours of power. In sixteen hours, our men will die. We have to get them from sixty amps down to twelve amps. That's our only hope."

"That's impossible. You can't run a vacuum cleaner on twelve amps!" someone shouted.

"We have to shut down everything," Arthur repeated firmly. "We have to kill the computer, the radar, the cabin heaters, the instrument displays. And we have to shut down the guidance system."

The room erupted as the controllers tried to understand what this meant.

"The guidance system!" somebody exclaimed. "They won't know where they're going without the guidance system!"

"How do you expect them to get home? The stars?"

"Look—the more time we waste down here, the more power they waste up there,"

Arthur said. "We have no choice. Their time is running out."

"That's the deal?" Kranz said.

"It's simple math."

"Okay." The flight director nodded. "First we burn and get them away from the moon. Then we shut down the power in the LEM. In the meantime, we're going to have a frozen command module up there. And in a couple of days we're going to have to power it back up using nothing but reentry batteries."

"That's never been tried."

"We're going to have to figure it out. I want people in our simulators. I want to find every engineer who ever worked on this mission. I need to know how many amps a light bulb draws. How many amps is in every computer chip? How many amps in the switches? Batteries, batteries, batteries. That's what we have to think about."

Within minutes, the halls and meeting rooms began to fill up with engineers, and the discussions began.

Meanwhile, up in space, the astronauts were getting ready to shoot the spacecraft out of moon orbit.

"No sweat, fellas. We blow this and we're

NASA's permanent solar-orbiting space museum," Jim said.

He glanced at the others and prepared to push the button to reignite the LEM's tiny engines. He hit the button marked "PROCEED."

In seconds, the Apollo spacecraft came alive again. The light from the LEM's thrusters glowed like a falling star, as they shot through the blackness like a ball from a cannon.

"Full thrust, Houston," Jack reported. "We're on our way."

As the astronauts watched, the moon faded and grew smaller. They were leaving the moon behind now. They were on their way . . . to somewhere.

 April 14
11:00 P.M.

By now, news of the Apollo explosion had spread around the world. Throughout Europe, Asia, and other parts of the globe, people waited for the latest reports, and in the U.S., the same television networks that had opted not to broadcast the astronauts' transmission were now carrying constant updates on the astronauts' condition. Along with the astronauts' families, it seemed everyone on Earth was praying for their safe return—Ken Mattingly included.

Ken Mattingly, the original Apollo 13 astronaut, should have been getting the measles by now, but he wasn't. It was a good thing. Ken knew the Apollo 13 spacecraft better than anyone else on the ground. When he strolled into the simulator building in Houston, the ground crew breathed a sigh of relief.

"Ken! Glad you're here," John Arthur called.

"I've been brought up to speed on what happened," Ken said. "But what do we really have left in the batteries?"

"No way to be sure."

"Well, we've got to get started on some shortcuts for power-up."

"Yeah. Do you know how short the cuts have to be?" Arthur asked.

"It's all in the sequencing. If we skip whatever we don't absolutely need, and if we turn things on in the right order, then maybe . . ."

"I agree. The engineers have taken a shot at

a new procedure. We've got to get you in the simulator."

Ken nodded. "I need it cold," he said. "Just like the command module. I want everything to be exactly the same. I want only what the guys up there will have. I'll need a flashlight."

A technician grabbed a big flashlight and handed it to Ken.

"This isn't the kind they have up there," Ken said, tossing it aside. "Like I said—I don't want anything they don't have on board!"

Ken took the heavy power-up manual and disappeared through the simulator hatch. Far above him, the astronauts were powering down the LEM. The moon's gravitational force would be taking over now, hurling them toward the earth. Ken didn't have a lot of time.

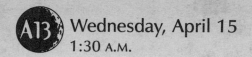
Cots lined the halls of Mission Control. A few exhausted controllers were asleep, while others stayed busy studying the flight manuals.

"We've got a serious problem here," another controller looked up from his monitor. "Those guys are breathing out too much air! Carbon dioxide is starting to build up. We have to filter that air out of there."

"What about the scrubbers?" someone asked, referring to the filters used to clean the astronauts' air. There were five of them in the LEM.

"The LEM only has enough scrubbers for two guys for a day and a half. We have three men breathing in there—and they've got to stay there for at least two more days."

"They're already up to eight on the gauge," the flight surgeon reported. "Anything over fifteen and they'll be breathing in enough carbon dioxide to impair their judgment, cause blackouts, and even cause brain damage."

"What about the scrubbers in the command module?" Kranz suggested.

The controller looked at him and shook his head. The command module had scrubbers. But they were square. The LEM used round ones. There was no way the *Odyssey*'s scrubbers could fit into the LEM's round holes.

Or was there?

Kranz gave his order. "Gentlemen, I suggest you invent a way to put a square peg in a round hole. We need a conversion kit, pronto. Let's come up with a way to make the scrubbers in the LEM square."

Like beavers building a dam, the men went to work. Suddenly, objects of all shapes and sizes appeared on the table. It was as if someone had pulled everything out of the Apollo spaceship and placed it there. Logbooks, towels, food bags, pressure suits, cables. Everything.

These were the things the astronauts would have to work with. These were the things they would use to make a round hole square.

Meanwhile, the Apollo astronauts were waiting. The lack of heat was causing a thin, wet layer of condensation to build up inside

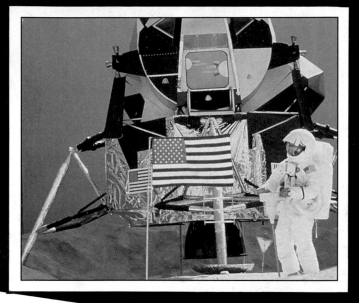

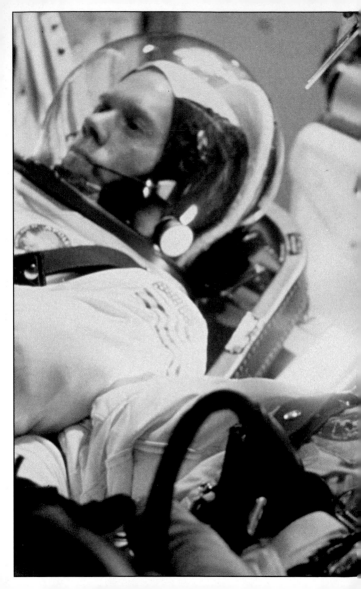

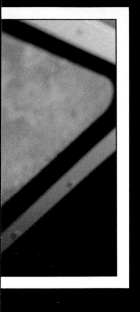

both the lunar module and the command module, covering every surface and fogging up their few tiny windows.

Inside the near-frozen command module, Jack was doing some figuring. Suddenly he tensed. Something was wrong.

Quickly, he floated into the lunar module and presented his figures to the others. "I've been going over the numbers again," he said in a voice filled with panic. "We're exceeding escape velocity. They've got us going way too fast. At this rate, we'll miss the earth's atmosphere and go into orbit around the sun."

"How do you come to that conclusion?" Fred sighed. He was not feeling well. His body was beginning to shake with fever.

"Look! I know how to add." Jack's voice was tense and angry.

"Some of the best scientists in the world are down there working on this thing," Jim reminded him.

"And if they made a mistake and there's no way to reverse it, do you think they'd tell us? There's no reason for them to tell us." Jack was starting to yell now.

"What do you mean they're not going to tell us?" Fred said. "That's crazy!"

"All I did was stir the tanks!"

"What was the tank reading before you hit the switch?" Fred asked edgily.

Jack glared at him. "Hey, don't tell me how to fly the *Odyssey*. They brought me in here and I did my job. They told me to stir the tanks."

"Jack, stop kicking yourself," Jim said, trying to calm his shipmates down.

"This is not my fault!"

"Nobody said it was, Jack," Jim said. "If I was in the left-hand seat when the call came in, I would have stirred the tanks, too."

"Well, tell Fred that."

Suddenly the radio crackled. "*Aquarius,* this is Houston," a voice said. "You might want to take a look at—"

A piercing whine interrupted him. The astronauts turned and searched the instrument panel in front of them.

"Uh, Houston," Jim said. "We have a carbon dioxide reading of thirteen here."

"My figures must have been wrong," Fred said. "I figured it for two people . . ."

"It's jumped four notches in ten minutes!" Jim exclaimed.

"We were expecting that, *Aquarius.*"

"It's nice to know that," Jim said angrily. "Now what do we do about it?"

"We're working on a procedure now."

"What am I supposed to do?" Jack muttered. "Hold my breath?"

Just then, an ecstatic technician burst into the Mission Control room. He ran up to Gene Kranz and handed him a bizarre-looking contraption. "This is what they're going to have to make," he gasped.

The next thing the astronauts knew, a voice was coming back over the radio. "Do you have the Flight Plan up there?"

"Affirmative," Jim answered.

"Well, we've got a few things for you to do."

"Roger."

"Rip the cover off."

The astronauts exchanged surprised looks. Then Jack smiled and ripped the cardboard cover off the bulky book.

As the technician radioed more instructions, the astronauts gathered parts.

"I need a sock," Fred said.

"A sock?" Jack asked.

"A sock. You know, foot, shoe, sock."

"Coming up." Jack pulled off his sock and handed it over.

"Now what am I supposed to do with this garment bag, Houston?" Fred said into the radio.

One by one, they found the things that they would need to make their air filter adapter. When it was finished, they taped it over the scrubber outlet in the LEM and listened.

"I can hear the air moving," Jack said.

"Breathe normally," Mission Control instructed them.

The astronauts took a deep breath, then let it out. In the cold air, they could see their breath—breath that could kill them if the new filter didn't work.

They stared at the carbon dioxide gauge and waited. Slowly, the needle on the gauge dropped down, then down even more, until it was well below the emergency level.

On the ground, long, relieved sighs passed through the halls and rooms of Mission Control.

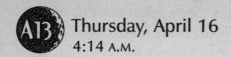
The astronauts were exhausted. They were filthy, and freezing, and on edge. The lunar module was a mess. Bags of urine, papers, leftover bits of hose, and all kinds of other things floated around their heads.

A voice crackled through the radio, shaking them out of a tortured half-sleep. Jim pulled himself forward and listened.

"Gentlemen, we've had another request from the flight surgeon. He'd like you all to get some sleep. He doesn't like the readings he's getting."

Jim fell back onto his couch. The words he had just heard made him angry. He knew he was tired. He'd been trying to sleep! He was sick of the flight surgeon and everybody else treating him like some science experiment. He'd show them.

Jim yanked up his shirt and glanced down at his chest and at one of the wires glued to his skin. It was that wire that allowed the flight surgeon to read what was going on in his body. It was that wire that told the flight surgeon that he needed sleep.

"See how he likes these readings," Jim muttered and yanked the wire off.

Down in Mission Control, the vital signs monitors flashed.

"I've just lost Lovell!" the flight surgeon cried.

But Jim wasn't done. He tore off the rest of the wires on his chest. "I'm tired of letting the entire world know how my kidneys are working," he announced.

Jack and Fred grinned. Then they ripped off their wires, too.

"We've had a dropout on your bio-med sensors," Mission Control reported.

"We aren't *wearing* our bio-med sensors," Jim replied happily.

The men in the spacecraft were smiling at each other now. They were people, not machines. And it was time that the world understood that.

"I'm losing all three of them!" The flight surgeon was still frantic.

But Kranz understood. The astronauts weren't dead. They were tired. "It's just a little medical mutiny, Doctor," he said. "I believe they're still with us."

Kranz moved over to his flight and guidance controllers. They were concentrating on the spacecraft's path. Something was wrong. Just as Jack had feared, the approach angle was off.

"At this rate, they'll nick the earth's atmosphere," one of the controllers explained. "If they come into it too shallow, they'll skip right off it and bounce into space. We'd better do something, or we'll never get them back. We need another burn to set them straight."

"*Another* burn?" Kranz muttered. The LEM's engines were designed to be fired only once. Could they burn them again? Did they even have enough power to do it?

"If they don't fire their engines," the controller went on, "they won't make it home."

Mission Control radioed the astronauts. "You're off course, *Aquarius*," the voice reported. "We have another course correction for you."

Jim groaned. Another correction? Forget about the spacecraft. Jim wasn't sure the astronauts themselves had enough energy for another course correction—Fred in particular. The shortage of drinking water had been especially rough on his kidneys, and the infection that had set in was hitting him hard.

"Are we bringing the guidance platform up on the computer?" Jim asked. The guidance platform would tell them exactly where they were, and point them in a straight line toward Earth.

"Negative on that, Jim," Mission Control said. "We can't spare the power."

The astronauts were stunned. They couldn't believe what they were hearing. Without the guidance computer, how would they know where they were going?

"You're kidding!" Fred said, his voice trembling from fever. "You mean we've got to do this blind?"

"I'm afraid so," Mission Control replied.

Suddenly, Jim's energy returned. He could do this. He knew it. He was a pilot, and now he was going to fly his ship. It had been a long time since he had done that. Computers had been doing it for him lately. Now, finally, it was *his* turn again.

"Okay, fellas," he said to Jack and Fred. "This is going to take all three of us. I'm going to line up the earth in the crosshairs and keep it there. We'll steer toward it. Jack, you keep track of the time. Watch those seconds very carefully. And look out the window every so often. Make sure you keep your eye on the earth in case I lose it in my sights."

"Got you," Jack said. His voice was high with excitement. No computers. It was great. They were pilots again.

"And Fred," Jim continued, "I can handle the start-stop and pitch-and-roll. Can you right us if we stray too far?"

"I'm with you," Fred said, trying not to sound weak.

"Fire when ready," Mission Control announced.

Jim's index finger hovered over the green button while Jack counted down the seconds.

"Minus four, three, two, one . . ."

"Ignition!" Jim said, as he hit the button.

Suddenly, the ship began to shudder and twist. Jim grabbed the pitch-and-roll stick and tried to steady the spacecraft.

"Steady, now," Fred whispered. He was struggling with the control that would keep them on course. "Come on, now."

"I'm losing it!" Jim cried, staring at the crosshairs. He glanced out the window and tried to find the earth. "It's slipping out of the crosshairs. Where is it? Where is it?"

Jack put his nose to the window and squinted. All around him stars were twinkling. But where was the earth? Suddenly, he had it. "It's there!" he shouted. "It's at seven o'clock!"

Jim glanced through the window again. He scanned the heavens. He couldn't see what Jack was seeing. He looked behind him and down, to where he would find the seven on a giant clock. At last, there it was. The earth. It was a magnificent sight.

"Got it!" he sighed.

Jim jabbed the red "STOP" button that would turn off the LEM's engines. The shaking stopped abruptly, with the center of the earth's day-night line lined up perfectly in his sight's crosshairs.

"We have shutdown, Houston," Jim said. "I hope we won't have to do that again."

By this time Ken Mattingly was in the simulator busy thinking about reentering the earth's atmosphere. How were the astronauts going to do it? It meant powering up the command module, and they didn't have much power left.

"Here's the order of what I want to do," Ken announced to John Arthur through the radio. "Power up the guidance system and communications. Then warm up what's needed to open the parachutes on reentry, and the command module thrusters."

"The thrusters will put you over budget on amps, Ken," Arthur answered.

"But the thrusters have been sitting at two hundred degrees below zero for four days!" Ken said. "Do you have any idea how cold two hundred degrees below zero is?"

"Fine," Arthur answered. "Then don't bother with the parachutes. Or lose something else."

"If the 'chutes don't open, what's the point?"

"You're telling me what you need. I'm telling you what we've got to work with at this point. I'm not making this stuff up."

"Well, they're going to need all these systems."

"We don't have enough power, Ken!"

"Okay, I am going to go back and try to find more power. There's got to be a way to do this. Let's start from scratch."

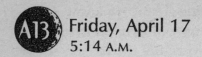
Inside the LEM, Fred was growing weaker every minute. Jim and Jack were very worried. They had to get Fred home—soon!

"Uh, Houston," Jim said into the radio. "We could sure use something resembling a reentry plan up here."

"Coming real soon, *Aquarius*."

"They don't know how to do it," Jack muttered.

"Maybe he's right," Fred weakly agreed.

"Look, Houston," Jim snapped, impatiently. "We can't throw this thing together at the last minute. So here's what you're going to do. You're going to come up with something, whatever it is, and we're going to go through it step-by-step so we don't have any foul-ups! I don't have to tell you we're all a little tired up here and we're not in a position to be making any snap decisions!"

"Ken Mattingly is working on it in the simulator right now, Jim."

"*Ken's* working on it?" It was the best news Jim had heard all day. He knew Ken could work out any problem. And he knew something else. If Ken was working on it, he must not have the measles.

Inside the simulator, Ken was trying to buy his fellow astronauts time. He was trying to find some extra power somewhere. But it wasn't easy. Where would it come from?

"There's got to be another way to look at this, John," he told John Arthur over his radio. "We know they've got some power in those LEM batteries, right?"

"Yeah?"

"And we have a cable that provides power from the command module to the LEM."

"Right. It's a backup for the LEM power supply."

"So reverse it," Ken said. "Reverse the flow and see if we can draw those last four amps from the LEM batteries before we cut it loose. In other words, we could charge the batteries in the *Odyssey* from the LEM. How much juice is left in the LEM?"

"They should be holding twelve or so."

"I don't need that much," Ken said. "I only need four amps. If you shut down almost everything, we've got it. We can defrost the command module and bring them home."

They quickly tried it out in the simulator.

"Okay," Ken said, as he worked. "How am I reading?"

"Fine so far," Arthur answered. "You're under the limit. Keep going."

"Now I'm bringing up the guidance," Ken announced as he hit a button.

"Ken?" Arthur said. "Is your computer on now?"

"Up and running. How do we look?"

"I think we got it, buddy!"

Ken hurried out of the simulator and into the Mission Control room. He slipped on a headset.

"*Aquarius*," he said, "this is Houston. Do you read me?"

"Read you, Houston," Jim said, grinning at the sound of his friend's voice. "Are the flowers blooming in Houston?"

Ken laughed. He knew what Jim meant. "No Jim," he said. "No flowers blooming yet—I don't have the measles. Is Jack in the LEM with you?"

"I'm here," Jack said.

"Jack, this is Ken Mattingly. Get yourself into the command module and get something to write on. You'll need a lot of paper."

When Jack was ready, Ken relayed numbers and instructions. Jack scribbled furiously. By the time they were finished, Jack was exhausted. He had been in space for almost a week now, most of it without sleep, and every inch of his body ached.

"Stand by, Ken," he said. "I'm having trouble reading my own writing."

"Don't worry about it," Ken told him. "I'll talk you through it. Turn breaker five on."

"There's an awful lot of condensation on the panel." Jack looked around at the drops of water clinging to every surface of the cold, dark ship. "What's the word on these things shorting out? Any chance of that happening?" He was worried about water getting into the wires. Even though the wires were coated and protected, one little crack, one loose seam into which water could leak, and the entire electrical system could short out and be destroyed.

"We'll take them one at a time, Jack."

Jack sat back and closed his eyes for a quick second. Then he opened them and went to work. "It's like driving a toaster through a car wash," he muttered as he flipped the first switch and held his breath. Nothing shorted out. "Breaker five on," he sighed, relieved.

Slowly, the command module began to return to life. Lights came on and reflected through the blackness.

"One more thing, 13," Ken called over to the astronauts still in the LEM. "While Jack's working on the power-up, you are going to have to transfer some weight over to the command module. We were expecting you to be toting a couple of hundred pounds of moon rocks, you know."

"Right, Houston," Jim said, a little sadly. It hurt to be reminded.

"Grab anything heavy and get it moving. We've got a lot to do before reentry."

Jim and Fred grabbed everything they could find—moon walk helmets and boots, manuals, the tape recorder, the TV camera— and tossed them down the tunnel toward the *Odyssey*.

"Okay," Ken called back to Jack. "Now, let's see if we can get that computer up and working. Go straight to nine in the list of instructions."

Jack read the instructions, winced, and hit a button. The computer pad on the front panel came to life.

"We got her back up, Ken!" Jack reported. "Wish you were here to see it."

"I'll bet you do," Ken laughed. "You can get ready to separate the service module now."

"Jim!" Jack called happily. "We're set to jettison the service module!"

"Roger that," Jim called back from the LEM. "On a three count. One, two . . ." Jim squeezed the thruster control. "Upward thrust!"

Jack hit the switches that released the service module. "We're loose!" he hollered, as the bulky service module floated free.

Fred and Jim swung around and looked out their windows. Inside the command module, Jack was looking too.

"I can't see it!" Jim shouted.

"There it is!" Fred said. "I see it!"

"I've got it!" Jack shouted from inside the command module.

Then Jim saw it too.

As if in slow motion, the service module floated past them—a huge, silver mass, as big as a battleship, shimmering in the sun's rays. As the astronauts watched, it rolled slightly, then rolled again.

"There's our venting problem," Fred said.

Where panel four should have been, there was a large, gaping hole. Trailing from the inside of the module were wires and hoses, spewing out like loose intestines.

Jim described what they were seeing to their colleagues on Earth. "Houston, we're getting our first look at the service module. There is one whole side of the spacecraft missing! A whole panel is blown out—from the SPS valve right up to our heat shield!"

Jim gazed through the window. He could see straight into the hole, into where oxygen tank two should have been. "It's really a mess, Houston," he continued.

No one was willing to say it. But the thought was in the mind of everyone on the ground and up in space. The service module had sat right over the *Odyssey's* heat shield. Had the explosion in the service module been close enough to damage the command module's heat shield? If so, there was little doubt that the command module would burn up when it tried to reenter the earth's atmosphere.

Unfortunately, there was no way to tell. At least, not before reentry.

Jim glanced around the *Aquarius*. Now that
the command module was fired up, it was
time to leave their little home. In a few minutes they would have to jettison this lifeboat
in order to prepare for reentry. Only the command module would splash down in the
Pacific. In front of them, the earth was a large
blue ball.

"Time to go, Freddo," Jim said, as he
turned toward his crewmate.

Fred was leaning against the bulkhead. He
looked so sick that Jim was shocked. Fred's
face was a strange, gray color, and his body
was shaking all over.

"You look awful!" Jim's voice gave away
his worry.

"Forget it," Fred said. "I'm all right."

"Can you hold on for a few more hours?"
Jim asked.

Fred nodded weakly. "As long as I have
to."

"When we hit that South Pacific, it's gonna
be eighty degrees," Jim reminded him.

Fred smiled as he thought about the warm weather.

"Why don't you help Jack out?" said Jim. "I'll finish up here."

Fred nodded and pulled himself toward the tunnel. He was so weak with fever that he could barely make it through.

"Jim," Jack called through the tunnel, "we're coming up on time to release the LEM."

Then Ken's voice came over the *Aquarius* radio. "Thirteen—we've got LEM jettison in sixty seconds. Have you got everybody in the *Odyssey*?"

Jim moved into the tunnel, slammed the hatch closed behind him, and floated toward the command module.

"Jim?" Jack hollered.

"I'm here." Jim floated to the front of the command module and headed for the left seat—the commander's seat. Whoever sat there flew the spacecraft.

But Jack was already there. Jim had forgotten. This was Jack's ship now.

"Sorry," Jim said. "Old habit." He looked at Jack for a moment, then moved aside. "It's yours to fly." Jim smiled, fully confident in his fellow astronaut.

"Thanks," Jack said, his eyes locking with Jim's. He nodded, and reached for the switch that would release the LEM.

With a tiny poof of air, the LEM separated from the command module, and *Aquarius* began to float away.

"We have jettison, Houston," Jack announced.

The three astronauts gazed through the window of the command module. Outside, the LEM was drifting farther and farther away. It was almost sad to see it go.

"Farewell, *Aquarius*," they whispered. "We thank you.

Jack shifted his attention to the thrusters. It was time to prepare for reentry. They needed a direct line in order to break through the atmosphere, and the line had to be perfect. If they shot themselves too high, they would burn up in the atmosphere and never make it through. If they shot too low, they would skip off the atmosphere and continue drifting through space.

"We're aligned for reentry, Houston," Jack said.

"Roger that, *Odyssey*. Expect you to hit in forty-five seconds," Mission Control replied.

But one controller was frowning at his screen. "Do you see what I see?" he asked the man in the next seat.

He did. The spacecraft was headed in too low.

The controller called Gene Kranz over. "Their trajectory is still a bit low," he told him. "Shall we tell the astronauts?"

"Anything we can do about it?" Kranz asked.

"No. Not now."

"Then they don't need to know." There was nothing, Gene Kranz knew, they could do now but pray.

 April 17
11:53 A.M.

Jim, Jack, and Fred couldn't see where they were going. Their instrument panel told them that they were approaching the earth at an increasing speed. But they couldn't see it, because they were flying in backwards.

They had to come in this way, with the earth's atmosphere at their backs, because the heat shield was also behind them.

The heat shield! Would it hold? Was it even there? A few more seconds, and they would know. The crew began to tense with excitement. They were almost home.

Down at Mission Control, they were excited too.

"Looking good, *Odyssey*. We'll have loss of radio signal in about a minute as you hit the atmosphere. We'll be talking to you again in three minutes. Welcome home!"

Gently, the sky outside of the command module curved from black to blue. A faint shimmer of pink lit the sky around them, then turned to orange as the ship touched the upper layer of the atmosphere. Seconds later, the orange turned to a fiery red as the temperature around the heat shield quickly rose to 5,000 degrees.

The astronauts lay back in their couches and closed their eyes. The condensation inside the command module was turning to rain now, drenching them. Outside, flames engulfed the ship, turning it into a falling comet of fire. Suddenly, as gravity gripped them once again, they were slammed back into their couches. The module raced toward

Earth, rolling back and forth, bouncing and shaking violently through the atmosphere.

"Any sign of them?" Ken asked after two minutes of radio silence.

Everyone in Mission Control was peering at the big blank screen on the wall. They shook their heads and stared straight ahead.

"Any news from the *Iwo Jima*?" Ken asked nervously. The naval ship, the *Iwo Jima*, was waiting in the Pacific to pick up the astronauts when they landed in the ocean. But they hadn't spotted anything either.

Throughout the world, people were watching and waiting too, gathered around their television sets and holding their breath. Their thoughts and prayers were with the astronauts.

"That's three minutes, *Odyssey*," Mission Control finally announced over the radio.

"*Odyssey*, this is Houston," Ken said. "*Odyssey*, do you read?"

"Where ARE they?" someone shouted.

"Four minutes, *Odyssey*," a controller said calmly. "Are you there?"

Still no answer.

"*Odyssey*, this is Houston. Do you read? Do you read me, *Odyssey*?"

Still, the world waited. But no one answered.

An Air Force cameraman spotted them first. He was leaning out of the bay door of a helicopter, scanning the sky through his camera.

"What's that?" he whispered, as he zoomed in on a small speck far above him. It was moving closer. It was silver. It was the *Odyssey*!

Suddenly, huge orange parachutes opened in the sky, like a wonderful peacock opening its tail feathers. Slowly, gently, the giant bird began to float toward the ocean. The astronauts were on their final leg toward home.

 April 17
12:07 P.M.

When the announcement came, the Lovell house went crazy. Jeffrey Lovell had been staring at the TV screen, waiting silently.

"The *Odyssey* has been spotted!" someone on the TV said in a voice filled with relief and happiness.

Jeffrey's mother put her head in her hands

and started to cry. The families of the other astronauts jumped up and down and cheered. People hollered and laughed and shouted. Everyone was hugging.

But Jeffrey Lovell didn't move. He stayed right there on the couch, and stared straight ahead. He was thinking—but he wasn't thinking about the moon, and he wasn't thinking about his moon rock. His father was safe. His father was coming home.

Inside the command module, the astronauts were grinning.

"Hello, Houston," Jim said into the radio. "This is *Odyssey*. Good to see you again."

"Roger that," Ken answered.

The *Odyssey* drifted toward the Pacific Ocean slowly, its orange tail feathers stretched out behind. The water was calm when they hit it. As the module bobbed gently up and down in the ocean, the men thought that they had never felt anything so wonderful.

The astronauts did not speak for several moments. They were listening for the whir of helicopter blades. When the sound finally reached them, they sat back and closed their eyes. They were all right. It was over now.

They kept their eyes closed as they waited

for the divers to descend from the helicopter and open their hatch. They were so tired. Fred's fever was higher now. And Jack's body ached in a way he had never thought possible.

Then the hatch opened. Through the door, they could see the blue Pacific. A diver's hands reached inside and helped Fred out.

"Glad to see you," he said.

"Glad to see you, too." Fred smiled weakly. "Very glad to see you."

As he watched Fred and Jack being lifted into the helicopter, Jim sat in the hatch and waited for his turn. Alone for the first time in a week, he glanced up at the whirling blades and smiled. They had been so lucky, he thought. People would think that sounded crazy. But they had been very, very lucky. Lucky that the explosion in the service module had happened on the way to the moon. And lucky that the LEM was still attached. It could have happened after they had landed on the moon, returned to the *Odyssey*, and jettisoned the LEM. They would have had no lifeboat then. Or what if it had happened while they were on the moon? They could have lifted off and docked with the command module. But the LEM would have been out of fuel, air, and power. It would have been useless.

A few minutes later, Jim was settled in the helicopter next to Jack and Fred. He looked down at the beautiful blue ocean and smiled. For a moment, he forgot that he had not stepped on the moon.

He had been gone for a week. It seemed more like a lifetime. But he was back now. And that was all that mattered.

 Afterword

It took a long time to figure out exactly what had gone wrong with Apollo 13. Everyone knew there had been a huge explosion. But they didn't know what had caused it. Finally, they discovered that the explosion had come from inside an oxygen tank in the service module. An electrical coil used to heat the tank had shorted out. And when the astronauts had tried to stir the oxygen up, the coil sparked and the tank exploded.

Some people called Apollo 13 a failure. The astronauts were supposed to land on the moon and they didn't. So it must have been a failure.

But Jim Lovell didn't think of it that way. He thought the mission had been a success. Yes, the goal of the Apollo program had been to reach the moon, to conduct scientific experiments on the moon's surface, to analyze the soil and rocks of that new frontier. But that was only one part of it. Another part was to see what people could do when they worked together. All those people on the ground. Those three men up in space. Thousands of people working together as a team.

Hadn't the idea been to work together to achieve a goal? And isn't that exactly what happened? They had brought the astronauts home.

* * *

This is a true story about real people. **Jack Swigert** went on to run for the Congress of the United States. He won, but sadly, he never made it to Washington. He died of cancer before he could take office.

Fred Haise never did get to walk on the moon. But he did go on to work for Grumman Aerospace, the maker of the spacecraft that had been his lifeboat.

Ken Mattingly did get another chance to fly to the moon, as the command module pilot for Apollo 16. He later became a member of the space shuttle team.

As for **Jim Lovell**, he never went into space again. He had flown four Apollo flights, and he decided that was enough. He retired from NASA in 1973.